# Drive-Through Christmas Eve

AND OTHER STORIES FOR CHRISTMAS

Written and Selected by
Richard and Elizabeth Raum

CrossLink Publishing
RAPID CITY, SD

Raum/CrossLink Publishing
1601 Mt. Rushmore Rd. Ste 3288
Rapid City, SD 57701
www.CrossLinkPublishing.com

Ordering Information:
Quantity sales. Special discounts are available on quantity purchases by corporations, associations, and others. For details, contact the "Special Sales Department" at the address above.

Drive-Through Christmas Eve/Raum—1st ed.
ISBN 978-1-63357-337-6
Library of Congress Control Number: 2020940552
First edition: 10 9 8 7 6 5 4 3 2 1

# Contents

*This is how God showed his love among us:*
*He sent his one and only Son into the world*
*that we might live through him.*

—1 John 4:9

# A Note to the Reader

T hank you for choosing our collection of Christmas stories. We've always enjoyed using stories as a way of celebrating our faith and telling others about God's amazing love in Jesus Christ. Now we are pleased to share these stories with you.

We wrote most of the stories to be told at Christmas Eve family services in churches where Richard was serving as the pastor. We encourage you to consider using the stories in this way. They are also appropriate for other church events, for family and classroom settings, and for personal reading, as well. It's a diverse collection, with stories varying greatly in plot, setting, and voice. They are suitable for all ages, although some will appeal more to adults than to children and vice versa. We also have included two classic stories ("The Christmas Chimes" and "The Holy Night") that fit the theme and character of the collection. We hope you will enjoy the stories and see the love of God shining through them.

Richard wrote some of the stories; Elizabeth wrote others. But we have worked so closely together over the years that in several instances we can no longer remember who originally wrote which ones. This is truly and fully a cooperative effort.

We are humbled and grateful that you've chosen to open this book. Enjoy. This Christmas season "may the God of hope fill you with all joy and peace as you trust in him, so that you may overflow with hope by the power of the Holy Spirit" (Romans 15:13).

—Richard and Elizabeth Raum

# Drive-Through Christmas Eve

Jim pulled into the drive-through and placed his order. "I'll have a burger. Make that a cheeseburger, small fries, small root beer, and an apple turnover."

Jim waited for a voice to acknowledge his order. None came.

"Excuse me. Did you get my order?"

Jim felt foolish speaking into a clown's face at a Circus Burger drive-through. After all, it was a holiday, and they were probably understaffed. He tried again.

"Excuse me again, please. Shall I pull up to the window, or do you want me to come in?"

"No, don't come in. You can't come in. We're closed." The voice belonged to a woman; she sounded young.

"Well, can I order something here?" Jim asked.

"No, we're closed. We close early on Christmas Eve. I must have forgotten to turn out the drive-through lights. Sorry."

"If you're closed, can you tell me what's open?"

"I think everything's closed."

"So, what am I supposed to do?" Jim instantly realized how foolish and pathetic he sounded. It certainly wasn't her fault the place was closed, or that he had been so busy at the paper he'd neglected to plan for dinner. Nor was it her job to find him a meal.

"Well," she said, "Quik Stops never close. You can always get something at one of them. I don't know of anyplace else."

"Thanks," Jim said. "That's what I'll do. Sorry I bothered you." He began to close his window, eager for the whole awkward exchange to end, when the voice crackled through the clown face again.

"Where are you from, anyway?"

"I'm from Buffalo, New York. My family's there, while I'm stuck here. Holiday or no, the paper must go to press."

"Buffalo? New York? That's where they have all that snow, isn't it? I bet you're used to having a real white Christmas."

"Sometimes, yes," Jim said, remembering the Christmas when he was eight and received his first downhill skis.

"I like it in the South, but I do miss the snow."

Jim felt embarrassed talking about home with a voice in the drive-through's clown face. Why had he said so much? True, he was lonely on this holiday night—lonelier that he'd ever imagined he would be. Was that the reason? Weeks earlier when he'd offered to work the city desk on Christmas Eve so that others could be home with their families, it hadn't seemed like a big deal. Now that the holiday was here, the idea of spending Christmas Eve alone in his apartment with an empty refrigerator made him feel sad and wistful. Talking to the clown face about Buffalo brought back powerful memories. They swirled around him as strongly as the lingering odor of hamburger grease.

"It's been nice talking to you," Jim said as he slipped the car into gear. "Merry Christmas to you and your family."

Before he could pull away, the clown voice crackled again. "I'm on my own, too. That's why I'm on cleanup tonight, so the others can go home. I'll be heading over to Calvary Baptist, the brick church across from the Legion Hall. That's my family, I guess. I'm supposed to say I'm a member of the Circus Burger family. The manager talks like that. But it doesn't really work that way."

"Of course not." Jim felt decidedly uncomfortable. He was about to say a final goodbye when she spoke again.

"How about you? Do you have a church to go to?"

"No, not here. I used to go to church when I stayed with my grandparents. I spent summers with them in Rochester. They always went to church, and they made me go. I never really minded." Until that moment Jim hadn't thought about church in years. He could almost smell the bouquet of roses from Grandma's garden that he helped her place on the Communion table on summer Sundays? Church reminded him of other flowers, the ones that overflowed the sanctuary on the day of Grandma's funeral. The people of that church had provided Grandpa with love and care ever since. That was why Jim hadn't felt compelled to visit. Now he wondered if Grandpa was sitting in his favorite pew this Christmas Eve. Did he wish Jim were sitting beside him?

"That sounds like the people at Calvary Baptist."

"Oh?" Had he actually said out loud the things he'd been thinking? The whole conversation was too personal, too uncomfortable. He had revealed things to the Circus Burger clown face that he'd never shared with his closest friends. He should drive away. That would end the conversation.

But he felt strangely drawn to the voice in the clown face. It was so open and vulnerable, yet poised and assured. She spoke with casual confidence.

"I guess I'm just not what you'd call a church person," he said at last.

"Sure, I understand where you're coming from. I used to be like that. But for a moment it sounded like maybe you were looking for something special, especially since it's Christmas Eve."

"Actually, I was looking for a cheeseburger and fries." The moment he said it, Jim wished he could take it back. He'd meant to be clever, not sarcastic. He knew he had failed. Finally, he said, "You've been very nice, but I've really got to go now. Merry Christmas."

"Same to you," she said.

Jim pulled away from the speaker. Then he stopped and looked back. The speaker was several inches behind him. Slowly he inched the car backwards until he was facing the clown.

"Excuse me," he said. "Are you still there?"

After a brief delay her voice came over the speaker. "Yes, I'm here. I'm waiting for you to leave before I cut off the lights and the speaker."

"I'm just wondering. That church of yours? You said it's called Calvary Baptist, across from Legion Hall?"

"Yes. We have two services tonight. The early one is over, but there'll be another one at nine, a candlelight service. It's very beautiful. You don't have to dress up or anything," she said quickly. "Everyone's welcome."

"Thanks." Jim slowly pulled away from the voice in the Circus Burger clown's face.

Later, he made his way to Calvary Baptist, parked in the Legion lot, entered the church and took a seat. He nervously glanced around the crowded sanctuary. Why had he come? Was it because of a voice in a clown's face?

Worship opened with a robust singing of "O Come. All Yet Faithful." Jim rose and sang along with the congregation, sensing that this was where he was supposed to be. He supposed those feelings would fade as soon as the service ended. But not so. He attended the next Sunday. There weren't nearly as many people there, but his sense of belonging returned. Each Sunday led to another. And another. Jim never found out who he'd been talking to at the drive-through that Christmas Eve, but as he became more and more involved in the church, he often thanked God for the faithful voice that invited him to church.

# Surrounded by Angels

I t had been twenty years since Brenda Van-
derhoof directed the Sunday school Christmas pageant. Her own children, who had
been in that pageant, were now grown with families of their own. Becky lived in Phoenix. She
only visited in the summer. Jason, his wife Ashley, and their two boys lived nearby. This year,
though, they would be spending Christmas in
Omaha with Ashley's family.

They had celebrated Christmas a week early.
Brenda made a Christmas dinner, the grandchildren opened their Christmas gifts, and the family talked about the upcoming trip. The boys were
excited. "But we can't take Walpole," ten-year-old
Ethan said. "Gran and Grampy are allergic."

"Really?" Brenda said, raising her eyebrows.

"And we're not sure that Walpole would appreciate a long car trip," Ashley added.

"Would you consider keeping Walpole here
for Christmas?" Jason asked.

How could she say no? Walpole was a lumber-
ing, lazy old mutt, not the kind of dog to disturb

the Christmas tree. Brenda noticed that when the tree lights started flashing, Walpole yawned, stretched, and turned around the other way. He spent most of the day asleep with his head resting on an old rag doll named Lester. Nothing bothered or excited Walpole as long as no one touched his beloved Lester.

Jason dropped Walpole off Thursday after supper. Christmas was on Saturday. "We'll get an early start tomorrow and be in Omaha in time for the Christmas Eve service," he said.

"Drive safely," Brenda called as he pulled away.

Once Jason left, the house felt strangely empty. Ray wasn't home from work yet. Walpole stretched out on the living room rug with the ever-present Lester. By the time Ray got home, Brenda had tripped over Walpole three times— her own fault, she confessed. "Walpole has taken over."

Ray went to work at the usual time on Friday; the company would close at three o'clock. Brenda had the day off. She was preoccupied with the church nativity pageant. She'd only agreed to take charge because everyone else claimed to be too stressed out with Christmas preparations.

When the Christian education committee proposed eliminating it—for just this one year—Brenda jumped in. "It wouldn't be Christmas without the pageant," she said. "It's a memory that these children will cherish." Not that Jason or Becky seemed to cherish the memory, but Brenda did. Maybe it was more for the parents than the kids. By the time she worked that out in her mind, it was too late. She had already committed.

Brenda packed up to leave for the church around 4:30. "I'll only have an hour to get the kids into their places for a final run-through," she told Ray. "Showtime is six o'clock. You'll come down for it, won't you?" she asked.

"Nope. Not this year." He settled into the recliner and yawned. "I've seen enough Christmas pageants to last a lifetime."

Brenda was disappointed, but she understood. "Then I'll leave you old dogs to enjoy a quiet evening."

"Don't you worry about Walpole and me," Ray said. "Might want to worry about the onion dip, though."

"Don't you dare!" she called as she put on her gloves. "I'm saving that for Christmas."

* * *

The Oliver twins and the Gillis girls were waiting on the front steps of the church. As soon as she unlocked the big wooden doors, they dashed inside and ducked beneath the pews or hid in the choir loft yelling, "Bet you can't find me!"

"Children!" Brenda yelled, although she hated to raise her voice in the sanctuary. Two boys and three girls came out of hiding, looking sheepish.

Soon, the rest of the church kids arrived. Most were dressed in appropriate costumes. But the Ellis boys, two of the three wise men, arrived directly from playing hockey wearing Dragons jerseys. "Costumes? Gosh, we forgot."

Brenda began sorting them into groups. "Shepherds to the right, wise men to the left, angels in the choir loft."

"What about me?" Madison Studwell said in a muffled voice. "I'm supposed to be Mary."

Brenda turned to look for Madison.

"I'm over here," she called. She was lying down on a pew with her ankle propped on the back of the pew in front. "I sprained my ankle tobogganing," she said.

"Can you walk?" Brenda asked.

"I'll have to. My parents said it wouldn't be fair for me to quit now. They said that Mary probably wasn't feeling so great either by the time she and Joseph got to Bethlehem."

"OK, then," Brenda said. "Just do your best."

Madison smiled. "I will." She limped to the back of the church, ready to begin her procession with Joseph.

Jessica Churchill, the head angel, took one look at the crowd of children and realized that she was the oldest one in the pageant. "What's going on here?" she asked. "My mother said all the kids my age were taking part. Was she tricking me?"

"Oh, Jessica. It's so good of you to help us out here. We need a head angel to keep the younger ones in order."

"Then I'll help out, but I'm not wearing an angel costume. No way." She slipped out of the satiny white robe, tossed the halo onto the organ, and stood tall in her "Save the Whales" sweatshirt.

When Brenda winced, Madison proclaimed: "Jesus loves all living things. He certainly loves whales." That was that.

Everyone was in the proper place and the rehearsal was about to begin when the children stopped listening. They stopped talking, too, but their eyes were not on her. They were staring at something behind her.

Brenda twirled around. A young woman carried a toddler down the center aisle. A boy of five or six traipsed after, clutching the hem of his mother's cloth jacket.

Brenda didn't recognize the family, and she knew everyone in town. "Can I help you?" she asked.

"I hope so. My car broke down. Right out front here. Is there a gas station nearby?"

"The Stop and Go sells gas, but they don't do repairs. There's nothing else open on Christmas Eve."

"Oh." The woman sank down into a pew. "Is it OK if we just sit here a minute and warm up? We'll stay out of your way. Once I figure out what to do . . ."

Brenda turned back to the children, but their attention remained focused on the strangers in their midst.

Jessica "Save-the-Whales" Churchill looked stricken. "Can't we help her?" she mouthed to Brenda.

Brenda looked from Jessica to the young woman shivering in the pew. Before she thought through what she was going to do, she said, "Why don't you call my husband?" She found an old grocery list in her pocket, pulled a pencil from the welcome pad at the end of the pew, and scribbled the phone number. "Tell him your problem, and he'll come help."

"Really?"

"He will," Brenda said, and she knew it was true. She felt bad about hauling Ray out on such a cold night, but she had no doubt he would come. Brenda turned back to the children. Jessica was smiling as she organized the angels.

Shortly after, parents, grandparents, and assorted relatives began to arrive. Brenda left a couple of parents in charge while she checked with the woman and her two little ones. "Did you make the call?"

She nodded. "He said he would come."

The five-year-old stared up at her. Brenda smiled. "Are you hungry?"

He nodded.

"They're fine," the woman said, but Brenda insisted that they follow her to the church kitchen. A big tray of cookies sat on the counter. (There were always refreshments after the pageant.) Brenda rummaged around in the church refrigerator and found a carton of milk. She checked the date. It was still good. "Milk and cookies," she said, and then she discovered a box of items that the church had set aside for the local food pantry. She poured the soup into a kettle, left the crackers on the shelf, and pulled spoons and bowls out of the cupboards. They were eating when Ray came clomping down the stairs. "Gotta go," Brenda called as she rushed back to the sanctuary. "Come and watch the pageant, if you want, while Ray fixes the car."

The congregation was singing carols when Brenda returned. The organist spotted Brenda, and when she waved he began playing "Away in the Manger." It was the signal for the pageant to begin.

Even without much of a rehearsal, the kids did a great job. The shepherds looked attentive and pleased to be there. The Ellis boys made perfect wise men, thanks to their grandmother, who delivered the costumes while Brenda was downstairs. Madison made a stunning Mary, looking lovingly at a cloth baby doll in the manger.

Even Jessica smiled. She had changed into a choir robe at the last minute and looked exactly like a head angel should look. She read the Bible story with sweet clarity and conviction. The congregation appeared delighted.

That's when Brenda noticed that the sanctuary door was slightly open. A dog wandered in. Brenda could have sworn—if she swore—that it was Walpole, Jason's dog. But what would Walpole be doing in church? He was home with Ray.

Except Ray wasn't home. He must have brought Walpole along to keep him company while he worked on the car. For a moment or two, Brenda relaxed. Walpole was a lazy old dog.

And then Walpole perked up. He peered down the center aisle. Something caught his attention. Walpole started running down the center aisle to the front of the church. He picked up speed as he went and snatched the doll right out of the manger!

"He's got *Jesus*!" Madison screamed. Other angels joined her: "The dog's got Jesus!"

The audience gasped. Robbie Berenson swung his shepherd's staff at Walpole as if to snare the dog's neck in the crook. Walpole backpedaled, panicked, and leaped to the left toward the Ellis boys. Gold, frankincense, and myrrh scattered in all directions.

Jessica, the appointed narrator, spoke calmly into the microphone. "Is there a dogcatcher in the house? Please, may I have your attention? Is there a dogcatcher in the house?"

Walpole had the doll gripped in his teeth. He shook his head back and forth, and then dropped it at the foot of a shepherd. It wasn't his beloved Lester after all. Walpole galloped back down the center aisle, slid out the door, and jumped into Ray's truck.

Everyone was laughing, except for one little girl who whimpered, "My dolly's covered with doggy drool," and Madison Stillwell, who dissolved in tears. Not only did her ankle hurt, but she also felt guilty for not keeping the baby Jesus safe.

Brenda wasn't laughing either. She had gone out of her way to volunteer to direct the pageant and give the congregation warm memories, and it had become a circus. At least she had the presence of mind to signal the organist to begin the last hymn, "Good Christmas Friends, Rejoice." The congregation rejoiced all the way home.

Brenda did not. She lingered in the sanctuary cleaning up and rehearsing how best to deal with Ray. She would ask him why he'd brought the dog to town, but she'd do it in such a way that he felt every bit of her anger. She was just turning out the lights when the young woman with the kids and broken car wandered inside.

"I just wanted to thank you," she said. "Your husband fixed the car. It's running like new, so we'll be on our way. But I couldn't leave without saying thank you."

"I'm glad he could help," Brenda said, and she meant it. Fixing the car was a good thing. Bringing Walpole to town was not.

"It wasn't just him, though. I want to thank you, too—you know, for the soup and cookies and the play."

"Oh, you saw that, did you? It wasn't quite what I planned."

"You mean with the dog?"

"That was funny," the little boy said. "I liked it."

"He did," his mother said. "I know it's not exactly like in the Bible, but we'll always remember tonight. It was like we were surrounded by angels. We came here needing help, and you helped us."

As Brenda drove home, words from the gospel of Matthew flooded into her mind  not the Christmas story, but the passage where Jesus tells the story of a king who thanks a group of people, saying: "For I was hungry and you gave me something to eat, I was thirsty and you gave me something to drink, I was a stranger and you invited me in, I needed clothes and you clothed me. . ." When no one remembers having done any of these things, the King replies, "Truly I tell you, whatever you did for one of the least of these brothers and sisters of mine, you did for me" (Matthew 25:35-36a, 40). The passage came to Brenda as a gift. Where moments before there had been anger, now she felt like singing.

When she reached home, Brenda burst in the door, hugged Ray, and patted Walpole. She set out a plate of Ray's favorite crackers and onion dip.

"Tonight?" he asked, a grin spreading across his rugged face.

"Tonight," she said.

Peace and joy filled Brenda's heart.

# The Christmas Chimes

Based on a classic story by Raymond McAlden

Once upon a time, in a country far away, a great cathedral towered over the city. It stood on the highest hill, and every Sunday great crowds climbed the hill to worship in the magnificent sanctuary. All who gathered there were amazed and thanked God that their city should be home to such an awesome structure. Huge stone pillars stood at the entrance. Beyond them lay the marble entrance, and beyond that an aisle so long that it was nearly impossible to see all the way to the altar. The organ was so loud that it sent music cascading out of the building into the hills beyond; on hearing it in distant places, some countryfolk thought it was thunder and that the skies were about to burst with a storm.

The great stone tower that held the chimes was even more amazing. It rose from the earth next to the cathedral and seemed to reach to heaven itself. Ivy sprouted on its gray walls, making it seem almost alive. At the very top of the tower were the Christmas chimes. According to legend the chimes played the most beautiful music in the world—better even than the great organ. Some folks claimed that the chimes sounded like angels; others said they sounded like strange winds singing through the trees.

People believed the chimes played only on Christmas Eve, and only then if a truly remarkable offering was laid on the altar. It had happened in the distant past when some great gift was given. People told stories of days gone by when the choir would be singing and suddenly the congregation would hear the bells from the tower, but no one still living had ever heard them.

Every Christmas Eve scores of people swarmed to the church hoping that their offering would make the chimes ring. Rich and poor, young and old brought gifts to the altar. Many brought money, of course. Others brought goods of one sort or another. They brought things that were extra, things they could spare. There was no doubt that these were useful offerings, but the chimes remained silent.

Among the people going to church that Christmas Eve were young Pedro and his little brother. They lived in a village far from the city, but on clear days they could see the great stone tower rising into the clouds. They knew nothing of the Christmas chimes, but they had heard of the beautiful Christmas Eve service held in the great city cathedral. "I have heard," Pedro said, "that it is the finest service in the land. The choir, they say, sings like angels, and hundreds of candles shine brighter than the noonday sun. Some even say that the Christ-Child comes down to bless the service. What if we could see him?" They had to go; they simply *had* to, and so they made a secret plan to travel to the city and attend the Christmas Eve service.

It was bitterly cold when they began walking to the city. Snowflakes filled the air, and an icy crust formed on the road to the city. The boys left mid-afternoon, for it was a walk of many miles. They slipped and slid along the road, holding hands in case they stumbled.

As darkness fell, the lights of the city came into view. The boys were about to enter the city gates when they noticed a dark form lying at the side of the road. They stopped to investigate.

The light was dim. Pedro pushed the lump gently with his foot. The lump moaned. He bent down for a closer look. Huddled beneath a dark shawl was an elderly woman. She had fallen just outside the gate. "Let us help you inside," Pedro said, but the woman was too sick and tired to respond.

Snow drifted around the woman as if it were a blanket and pillow. Soon, Pedro realized she would be sound asleep, and given the cold, it was a sleep from which she would never awake. He knelt down and tried to rouse her but without success.

He looked somber. He turned to his younger brother and said, "You'll have to go on alone."

"Alone? But you want to attend the services even more than I do. You said it was the finest service in the land."

"That is true, and I would love to go, but I do not have a choice. I must stay here. This poor woman will freeze to death if we leave her here, but if I stay, I can rub some warmth back into her. Perhaps I can coax her to eat a bit of the bread that I put in my pocket. When the service is over, you can bring help."

"I cannot leave you. I will stay, too," Little Brother said.

But Pedro was firm. "There's no need for us both to miss the service. You must see and hear everything twice, once for yourself and once for me. And, if you get the chance, slip up to the altar and leave this little silver coin there for me. It is the offering I planned to give the Christ-Child."

Now that he had a task to perform, the little brother agreed.

"But do not forget where you left me, and please forgive me for not coming with you," Pedro said.

The younger brother hurried into the city and followed the crowds to the cathedral. Pedro remained alone in the dark, gently rubbing the woman's hands and feet and covering her with his own thin jacket.

Little Brother entered the great sanctuary on tiptoe, straining to see everything so that he could give Pedro a detailed report. He noted the beautiful greens decorating the chapel, the hundreds—if not thousands—of candles placed on every window ledge and in every available nook. He noticed the colorful wraps and shawls worn by the worshippers and the excitement evident in the way they walked and talked with one another.

When the service began, he joined a thousand others in the familiar carols. The music seemed to lift his feet off the stone floor. Oh, how he wished Pedro could have come. It was as if the music carried him to Bethlehem and back.

As the service ended, everyone rushed forward to place the offerings on the altar. There were jewels and baskets full of gold. A renowned painter brought one of his masterpieces, and a basket weaver delivered a basket so delicate that it looked to be woven of silk. Last of all, the king walked down the aisle, lifted the crown from his head, and placed it on the altar.

A hush fell over the crowd. Surely now the Christmas chimes would ring. The people listened. They waited. But the chimes remained silent.

The crowds began to drift away.

Just when it seemed that nothing would awaken the Christmas chimes, they came to life. Something had caused the long-silent bells to ring.

People surged forward. Was it the artist's painting? The silk basket? The king's crown?

No. It was none of these. What the people saw was a small boy placing his brother's meager silver coin on the altar. The bells sang that night not for the coin—nor for the many riches that the people had offered. No, they sang for Pedro, the little boy's brother, who had remained outside in the cold in obedience to Christ's command to "love your neighbor as yourself." It was surely the greatest gift. For as Jesus said, "Dear children, let us not love with word or tongue but with actions and in truth" (1 John 3:18).

# Saint Washburner

On Christmas Eve Sarah sat in church with her mom and dad. She tried to stay awake during the service, but the combination of last-minute shopping and the drone of Reverend Emerson's voice as he read the familiar Christmas Eve Scriptures caused her head to droop in a pantomime of prayer. She felt herself letting go, giving in to an overwhelming urge to sleep. Her mother must have noticed, because she gave Sarah a firm jab in her left side. Sarah forced her head up, opened her eyes, and glanced at the choir.

Miss Washburner sat in the front row of the choir, as usual: tall, proud, and bound to be off-key. The aging spinster smiled directly at Sarah, as she always did. Miss Washburner had been Sarah's Sunday school teacher in both first and fifth grades. Sarah remembered those early lessons vividly. Miss Washburner had one message for the first graders, and she repeated it over and over again. "Jesus loves me," she would say, and pointing to each and every child individually, she would add, "and you, and you, and you." Then she would lead the children in singing, "Jesus loves me / this I know / for the Bible tells me so." There was always a Bible story, and the lesson ended as the children colored a picture of whichever Bible story Miss Washburner had chosen for that day. Whenever Sarah smelled crayon wax, she remembered Miss Washburner's first-grade Sunday school class.

In fifth grade, the message changed, but its constant repetition continued to be Miss Washburner's style. "Children," Miss Washburner would ask at the beginning of each class, "What is the chief end of man? (And that means all of us—boys and girls, too—and remember that 'end' means 'what we should be doing with our lives')."

By the third week the children knew enough to respond: "Man's chief end is to glorify God and to enjoy him forever."

"It may have been written in 1647, children, but the Westminster Catechism was good enough for generations of children, and it is good enough for you. When I was a child," she would add, "I had to memorize the entire shorter catechism. Count yourself lucky that you have to learn and understand only this one important question."

By the end of the year every child in the class knew what Miss Washburner meant when she said "man's ('and that includes all of us') chief end is to glorify God."

For Miss Washburner, using your talent to glorify God included singing in the choir, even if you were slightly tone-deaf. Sarah watched as the choir rose for the anthem. At least God has the power to forgive our iniquities, Sarah thought, and Miss Washburner's voice certainly qualified as one! Sarah smiled courteously at Miss Washburner, who already appeared to be lost in a trill, carried away by her attempt to glorify God.

Jeannie, who was sitting across the aisle, winked at Sarah and held a church bulletin to her face to hide a snicker. Often, when they were younger, the girls had tried to imitate Miss Washburner's strained notes, only to collapse in hysterics. "One of these days," Jeannie used to say, "She's going to shatter a stained-glass window."

Only a few hours earlier Saint Washburner (as Sarah and Jeannie had come to call Trinity Church's self-selected saint) had swooped down on Sarah and Jeannie as they did some Christmas shopping at Walmart. The girls were checking out new shades of lipstick when Miss Washburner hailed them. "So," she boomed loudly enough to turn heads, "how are my two prize Sunday school students? Serving the Lord, I hope." And she chuckled as she trouped on. Sarah expected to hear the clunk, clunk, clunk of Miss Washburner's black orthopedic shoes, but she heard instead Miss Washburner's hearty greetings to each and every shopper.

"She's probably on her way to feed the hungry," Jeannie said. "I wonder if even the 'down and out' laugh at her polyester dresses and sensible shoes. She's such an antique."

Sarah turned to see if anyone had overheard, but the girls seemed to be alone. As weird as Miss Washburner was, Jeannie's jokes sometimes made Sarah feel uncomfortable.

Miss Washburner was paying the cashier when Sarah and Jeannie carried their own purchases to the cash register. Jeannie nudged Sarah. "Will you look at that?" she said and pointed at Miss Washburner's purchase: a pair of sturdy black leather work boots. "What on earth is she going to do with those? Her 'sensible shoes' are bad enough."

"A gift?" Sarah asked, but Jeannie merely shrugged.

It was the image of Miss Washburner wearing those sturdy leather work boots that appeared to Sarah now as the choir sang. Why would Miss Washburner need work boots? These were not the gardening variety. They were the steel-toed kind, designed for construction workers.

After the anthem, the choir settled back into their seats, and Sarah stopped daydreaming. Pastor Emerson rose and motioned for Miss Washburner to join him at the pulpit. Miss Washburner hesitated. Was it possible that the robust "saint" was embarrassed?

The pastor began. "We come here tonight to celebrate the birth of Christ, but in a larger sense of course, we are celebrating Christ's life and teachings. Christ called us the 'light of the world.' Recall with me the words from Matthew 5:15-16. 'Neither do people light a lamp and put it under a bowl. Instead they put it on its stand, and it gives light to everyone in the house. In the same way, let your light shine before others, that they may see your good deeds and glorify your Father in heaven.' On this special night, you see before you someone whose light shines for all of us."

Miss Washburner blushed.

"Our dear sister in Christ, Evelyn Washburner, has volunteered to help the victims of the hurricane which ravaged the coast of Puerto Rico this fall. A call came to the church office this week, asking if we could send volunteers and supplies. Evelyn was quick to respond. She leaves at the end of the week."

Pastor Emerson turned to Miss Washburner. "Our prayers go with you, Evelyn," he said. "And anyone who would like to donate blankets to the cause may drop them off at the church office this week."

Sarah noticed many people writing notes to themselves. They would go home and check the closet for a spare blanket or two to send along with Miss Washburner, so she could pass them on to the hurricane victims.

Pastor Emerson led the congregation in prayer. Sarah prayed for Miss Washburner and for the hurricane victims. She could picture a shining Miss Washburner wearing her steel-toed work boots, her arms filled with blankets, which she would distribute to children in Puerto Rico.

After the congregation sang "Silent Night," a crowd gathered around Miss Washburner. Sarah avoided looking at Jeannie. She knew that Jeannie would be eager to joke about Miss Washburner and her trip to Puerto Rico. "Poor kids," she might say, "not only a hurricane, but Miss Washburner, too." No, Sarah didn't want any part of that.

Sarah left the sanctuary and waited for her parents in the hallway. She surveyed the bulletin board and noticed a letter posted there. "To the saints of the church. In the aftermath of the devastating hurricane, we need your support and prayers. . ." Sarah didn't read further. "To the saints," the letter had begun. Saint Washburner. Suddenly it all made sense.

# "Bring a Torch, Jeanette, Isabella"

**Inspired by a Carol**

"Jeanette, Jeanette. Do you hear that?"

"Hear what?" Jeanette asked, yawning and turning over in the bed. "I don't hear anything. Go back to sleep."

"No, listen. Listen closely."

The two girls lay silently, each in her own bed in the tiny upstairs bedroom. It was chilly. The old French farmhouse did not have heat upstairs, and the fireplace in the kitchen below had grown cold. The sisters snuggled under the covers.

"There it is again. Did you hear it this time?"

"Yes. I think I did."

There was no doubt about it: a strange noise was coming from the barn.

"What do you think it is, Isabella?"

"I don't know. Maybe we should wake Papa."

"Oh, no. He was up all last night helping that old cow get better, and he was out cutting wood all day today. He didn't even make it home in time for supper. He needs to sleep.

"Shh. . .there it is again." And she was right. That strange sound came again. Someone was in the barn. But who?

Jeanette stepped out of bed and shook with cold. "I'm going to see," she said.

"By yourself? You can't go to the barn by yourself in the middle of the night."

Jeanette had already wrapped herself in a warm shawl. "Then come with me."

"But I'm afraid to come. And it's cold."

"Then stay here if you wish, but I'm going."

And so it was that the two girls, dressed in their warmest shawls, tiptoed down the steps, determined not to wake Papa or Mama. Jeanette went first, holding her sister's hand, and gently encouraging her to cross the yard to the barn.

They found the barn door open, ever so slightly. The cows snored, the chickens scratched, and the donkey poked his nose against the stall door.

"The animals are awake," Isabella said. And then she heard people talking. She pulled back. Who could it be?

"Hello? Hello?" Jeanette said in her deepest, strongest voice. But she was scared, so the words sounded more shaky than sure. "Is anyone there?"

"Yes. There are two of us," a man said.

"Three," a woman corrected.

The girls squinted into the darkness. They could barely make out the form of a man standing in the corner. A woman sat on a bale of hay beside him.

"We didn't mean to disturb you," the man said. "We'll soon be on our way."

And then there came a sound so unexpected that the girls would remember it forever. Many years later they would tell their grandchildren about what had happened that night, and when they got to this part of the story, they'd act surprised all over again. No matter how many times they told the story, they got excited when they said, "It was a baby. We heard a baby cry!"

"Our son," the man said. "He was just born. My wife and I ducked into your barn to get out of the cold and to rest. And the baby chose your barn for his birthplace."

"Come, girls. Come and see," the woman said. She sounded young, only a few years older than Jeanette.

The girls hesitated, but only for a moment, before carefully making their way to the corner where the woman sat. They peeked at the baby who lay in his mother's arms. His eyes were closed; he was sleeping.

"He's lovely," Jeanette said.

"So sweet," Isabella added.

"Do you girls have a mother in the house? Do you think she would be willing to come out and help my wife?" the man asked.

"Oh, yes! She won't mind at all," Jeanette said, and she whirled around and raced out the barn door as Isabella struggled to catch up. "A baby!" she yelled as she ran. "A baby in the barn!"

The girls' mother hurried to the barn. The girls followed. So did Papa.

"What's this about a baby?" he growled. "What's a baby doing in the barn?"

Mama took control at once. "We need some things right away." She told papa to get a blanket. "Get several," she added. "And water. We need water. And something to eat. Our visitors must be hungry."

"And one of you girls," she said. "Bring a torch so we can see in here. Hurry!"

"I'll do it," shouted Isabella. "I'll go!" shouted Jeanette. They both yelled at once.

"Hush! The child is sleeping. Both of you do it. But be careful. And be quiet. Don't wake the baby."

In a few minutes everyone was together again in the barn. Papa had gathered blankets, water, and food. The girls had brought a torch so there was light. And in the flickering light they saw more clearly the beautiful baby sleeping on a tiny bed formed of hay. His mother and father looked on proudly.

"What a difficult life they must have," Jeanette whispered to Isabella. "Imagine having a baby in a barn without family or friends to help."

"What do you mean?" Isabella whispered back. "They have us. We're their friends. We're almost like family."

"Yes, we are," Jeanette agreed.

It was quiet in the barn. . .and peaceful. . .and calm.

The three visitors left the next day. They never said where they were going, and the girls never knew what happened to the baby. But they always imagined that "their" baby became special in some way. After all, he had come into their lives as a totally unexpected gift. They were forever glad that the barn had been there, and that they'd been there, too.

From that night on, the girls lived with great joy. They were seldom grumpy or gloomy or mean; for they knew that in this world amazing things do happen. Some call them miracles.

The Carol: *Bring a Torch, Jeanette, Isabella*

*Bring a torch, Jeanette, Isabelle!*
*Bring a torch, to the stable run.*

*Christ is born. Tell the folk of the village*
*Jesus is born and Mary's calling.*
*Ah! Ah! Beautiful is the mother!*
*Ah! Ah! Beautiful is her child.*

*Who is that, knocking on the door?*
*Who is it, knocking like that?*
*Open up, we've arranged on a platter*
*Lovely cakes that we have brought here.*
*Knock! Knock! Knock! Open the door for us!*
*Knock! Knock! Knock! Let's celebrate!*

*It is wrong when the child is sleeping,*
*It is wrong to talk so loud.*
*Silence, now as you gather around,*
*Lest your noise should waken Jesus.*
*Hush! Hush! See how he slumbers;*
*Hush! Hush! See how fast he sleeps!*

*Softly now unto the stable,*
*Softly for a moment come!*
*Look and see how charming is Jesus,*
*Look at him there, his cheeks are rosy!*
*Hush! Hush! See how the child is sleeping;*
*Hush! Hush! See how he smiles in dreams!*

# Owen

Owen is in a wheelchair, partially paralyzed from a childhood accident. He's always been *slow*, which is the polite word in his hometown of Ashford, New Hampshire, for someone with serious intellectual disabilities. Ashford is about an hour's drive north of Concord. If Owen lived anyplace else, someone might take advantage of his disabilities and harm him or rob him, but everyone in Ashford knows Owen, protects him, and watches out for his well-being.

Owen lives with his unmarried sister Gloria in a run-down trailer court behind Ashford Elementary. Gloria works in the school cafeteria. Owen has always worked for himself.

Every afternoon he sets up a card table, puts a white linen cloth on it, and covers it with items to sell. He sells candy bars and baseball cards, pencils and pens, erasers, key chains, refrigerator magnets, stickers—anything that is small and light and that school children are likely to buy. After all, children are his primary customers: children on their way home from school and children playing after school.

On nice days, Owen sets up his card table in front of Ashford Community Church next to the school. On cold or wet days, Owen moves the table inside the narthex of the church, and on Friday nights in winter, when the Ashford Cats play home basketball games, Owen sets up his table by the coat room at the high school.

Owen keeps his money in a cigar box, and customers make their own change. Maybe he's been cheated once or twice over the years, but it couldn't have happened often because everyone in the neighborhood keeps an eye on Owen. If a kid stole money from Owen, the other kids would see to it that the thief was dealt with promptly and the money returned. Children have always loved and protected Owen because he is their friend. He is like a child: simple and guileless and able to appreciate the ways of children, even those ways that annoy most adults. Children grew up buying items from Owen, and on Christmas parents throughout the neighborhood have always known that the shoelaces, thread, combs, and erasers they receive as gifts were selected from Owen's table.

All this changed, however, when the new pastor came to Ashford Community Church. Pastor Mick was an enthusiastic and hard-working young pastor. He preached practical, down-to-earth sermons, visited shut-ins, stopped for morning coffee and caramel rolls at the café, and cheered for the Ashford Cats. Everyone liked Pastor Mick except for one thing: the new pastor didn't want Owen selling trinkets in the church narthex.

Folks had different explanations for Pastor Mick's attitude. Some said they thought it was a matter of Bible teaching. They claimed that Pastor Mick believed Jesus's opinion on the matter was stated once and for all when he overturned the tables of the money changers at the temple. Others insisted that Pastor Mick had attended a workshop on legal problems in the church, and that his opposition to Owen had to do with "product liability" and things like that. Some argued that Pastor Mick felt he couldn't leave Owen alone in the church building, and that he didn't want to be confined to the office every afternoon. Some said that Pastor Mick, who was an extremely logical man, reasoned that if one person was permitted to run a business in the church, then anyone should be permitted and there would be no end to it. People seemed to agree that the pastor simply found Owen's after-school sales annoying.

Although no one knew exactly what was said, news spread quickly through town when Pastor Mick met privately with Gloria in the school kitchen after lunch one day in early December.

He told her that Owen would no longer be permitted to set up his table in the church narthex.

The people didn't agree with Pastor Mick about this, but they agreed that his reasons, whatever they were, must be good. He was, after all, the pastor, and they trusted him to do what was best for the church. It hadn't been easy in recent years to convince capable young pastors to come to Ashford, and they surely didn't want to risk driving him away. Owen would always be with them no matter what was said or done, but Pastor Mick might pick up his family and leave if he felt besieged with criticism. Although folks felt bad for Owen, no one knew what to do about it or how to go about changing it.

The whole issue had pretty much passed from everyone's minds when they gathered for the seven o'clock family service on Christmas Eve. This early service was planned and led each year by the Sunday school. A more serious candlelight Communion service would be held at eleven. The theme of this year's early service was "O Come, Let Us Adore Him." Each class would sing a song or offer a brief reading from the chancel steps or perform a skit on ways to show love and adoration for Christ.

"We show we adore him when we come to church," the preschoolers recited.

"We show we adore him when we pray to him," the kindergarten and first-grade class said.

"We show we adore him when we give money to help our mission workers in other countries teach people about him," the second through fourth graders announced. Then they performed a skit featuring a missionary teacher talking to people in colorful robes about the birth of Jesus.

"We show we adore him when we take care of his good earth," the fifth and sixth graders began. Then they acted out bringing cans and newspapers to recycling bins, picking up trash, and so forth.

The congregation sang a carol or two each time one class returned to their pew and the next class came forward, so the service took a full hour. Everyone looked forward to the final scene because the junior high school class could always be counted on to do something creative and fun.

At the appointed time in the service, while the congregation was singing the final verse of "It Came Upon a Midnight Clear," junior high class member Jennifer MacCroskey stepped to the pulpit and said, "We show we adore him when we know and rely on the love God has for us." (John 4:16)

Then a most remarkable thing happened. While a group of junior high students sang "O Little Town of Bethlehem" from the back of the sanctuary, Mary and Joseph slowly made their way down the center aisle. Meredith Lindemann, a petite seventh grader with bright red hair and large purple-rimmed glasses, played the role of Mary. But the sight of Joseph surprised the congregation. Many gasped at first, and then after the initial murmurs, they remained absolutely silent. Owen, dressed in a plaid flannel bathrobe and wearing a Red Sox cap, had become Joseph. He held the baby Jesus doll gently to his heart.

Jeff Carlisle, an eighth grader, wheeled Owen down the aisle. Meredith, as Mary, walked beside Owen.

Class members took turns reading from Scripture and speaking about the importance of acceptance and love, but few in the church listened to what was actually said. Everyone focused on Owen, sitting with such quiet dignity in the midst of the nativity scene at the front of the church.

No one seems to know exactly what happened next—or maybe those who know aren't saying—but when school reopened on January 2, there was Owen, back in the narthex of the church with his card table of goods.

Pastor Mick stopped by The Coffee Cup that morning, and someone good-naturedly said to him, "I suppose after a while every Christmas gets to be pretty much the same for a pastor, eh?"

Pastor Mick smiled and said, "No, actually every Christmas seems to teach me something new or allows me to see something old in a new way."

Owen is still in a wheelchair, partially paralyzed from a childhood accident, and he'll always be a bit slow. But Owen, child of God, has a special place in the hearts of all who live in Ashford, Pastor Mick included.

# The Sweetest, Brightest Moment of the Year

When Fr. Kevin Poindexter, then Associate Pastor at St. Aloysius, experienced a second heart "episode" last summer, the Bishop arranged for his transfer to the Diocese of Marquette, far from the mean streets of Detroit. Fr. Kevin had spent his entire life in the city. He was tempted to turn down the transfer. What did he know of life in isolated rural communities? How could he meet the needs of people so different from his Detroit congregation? But he eventually agreed that it was time for a change; otherwise, he would be risking serious illness, and then he'd be of no use to anyone.

Actually, his first six months at the White Pine Cooperative Parish had gone surprisingly well. Fr. Kevin officiated mass at Kloppers each Saturday night. On Sunday morning, he held two services, one at Rogers, where he lived, and the other at Reuger. On alternate Sunday evenings, he conducted mass at tiny Tornio. As exhausting as this worship schedule sounded at first, along with hospital visits, CCD classes, and council meetings, Fr. Kevin actually found the rhythms of small-town life relaxing and enjoyable. He quit smoking, renewed his daily devotional life, and took up watercolor painting.

The crisp nights and red leaves of autumn convinced him that his new parish wasn't such a bad place to be after all, although it was far different from life in the city. St. Aloysius had been a rough parish, filled with crime and drugs. People who were homeless slept on the rectory steps. Fr. Kevin spent his time not only in the church, but in the streets, in the schools and stores, in the bars and barbershops. The people appreciated his tireless efforts to help them, and they openly expressed their affection. People smiled at him, said "thank you," and the children gave him hugs. Many thanked him with cards and notes or delivered homemade split-pea and ham soup to the rectory. School children gave him pictures they painted, and though he often could not identify whatever it was they had intended to paint, he was touched by their thoughtfulness. He felt encouraged by these expressions of love and appreciation.

However, that was not the case in the isolated communities of White Pine Parish. The ancestors of these strong-willed Catholics, immigrant people from Germany and Czechoslovakia and the Ukraine, had squeezed a living out of the unforgiving north woods through grim determination and steely perseverance. That spirit of tough resolve still prevailed. His new parishioners were solid, decent people. They were cordial, but nothing more. He'd seen them laugh and sing and dance robustly, but they were strangely awkward and sluggish when it came to showing care and concern for him or one another.

As Fr. Kevin walked from the rectory to the church at Rogers for the Christmas Eve mass, his mind drifted back to St. Aloysius. He wondered how the services there were going. He considered Christmas Eve the sweetest, brightest moment of the year. He knew that the troubles his people carried would not be lifted magically for Christmas, and in some cases might become worse, and yet the timeless truth and beauty of this evening never failed to restore hope within him. Would that happen on this night?

He carefully placed a white stole with gold braid around his neck, a stole given to him as a farewell gift from the St. Aloysius day care staff and now being worn for the first time. Fr. Kevin wondered if he would ever feel as accepted here as he had felt in Detroit. He reluctantly admitted to himself that he felt lonely and isolated. "Everlasting Father," he prayed, "let me lean on you with all my heart instead of relying on my own imperfect understanding. You are my strength and my shield."

On Christmas Eve the sanctuary at Rogers, the largest in the parish, was packed. All four congregations had come together for the Christmas Eve mass. Many faces were new to Fr. Kevin. They were, he assumed, relatives and former residents home for the holiday. He greeted those he knew and welcomed those he didn't, although he wondered what they had been told about the new priest. Some of the comments had made their way back to him:

"That new priest of ours has city ways."

"He tells jokes in his homilies and laughs right out loud at his own jokes."

"Sometimes he loses his place in the liturgy."

"The Sunday before the Northern Trails Regional Playoff football game he actually prayed for the team."

Yes, Fr. Kevin knew what people were saying about him! They never said, "Good evening, Father," or "How are you, Father?" It was always merely "Father" with a stiff nod of the head.

As he looked out over this sea of firm faces, Fr. Kevin resolved to bring as much enthusiasm as he could to the occasion. And he did. Even so, the congregation recited their responses sparingly, as though each had been allotted a set amount of enthusiasm at birth and no one wanted to waste it in church. As he led the liturgy, his mind kept returning to St. Aloysius and the pleasure he used to feel when children wandered around the sanctuary, teenagers whispered in the balcony, and the worship team tuned guitars during prayers. He enjoyed that lively spirit—the noise and commotion—and the people. He was delighted that they seemed to enjoy him in return.

Finally, the moment came for worshippers to come forward to the Communion table. "Happy are those who are called to His Supper," Fr. Kevin pronounced, but as he spoke familiar words of invitation, they sounded strangely empty and deceitful. Why wasn't he joyful? It was Christmas Eve!

As was his practice, Fr. Kevin stood at the door as the congregation left, and to each he smiled with hearty good cheer, although it felt somewhat forced. "Merry Christmas! Merry Christmas, George! Merry Christmas, Anita! Has your family arrived from Denver yet? Merry Christmas, Wayne! How's that knee doing? Merry Christmas!"

It wasn't until everyone had left that he noticed that someone had placed a sign on the table near the entrance. The departing congregation had blocked his view, but now he could see more clearly. Fr. Kevin moved over for a close look.

He read the sign, and then rubbed his eyes. Could it be? In black marker, someone had written: *Merry Christmas, Father Kevin!*

For him? He glanced at what appeared to be gifts. Some were wrapped in Christmas paper or hidden in paper bags; others had no hint of fancy or decorative detail. There were fruitcakes, a bottle of bourbon, and trays of Christmas cookies. There were books and pens, socks, special-blend coffee, and gift certificates for McDonald's. On top of the pile, perched at a jaunty angle, sat a Detroit Red Wings cap.

Fr. Kevin bowed to pray, barely holding back tears. Here, at his feet, was an outpouring of love and thankfulness, unexpected, but oh, so appreciated. It wasn't that he needed gifts; what he needed was encouragement, and here it was as if in answer to his prayer.

Folding his hands shakily in front of him, he spoke with joy and gratitude the prayer of St. Francis:

> *Lord, make me an instrument of thy peace:*
> *Where there is hatred, let me sow charity;*
> *Where there is injury, pardon;*
> *Where there is error, truth;*
> *Where there is doubt, faith;*
> *Where there is despair, hope;*
> *Where there is darkness, light;*

*And where there is sadness, joy.*
*O, Divine Master, grant that I may not so*
*much seek*
*To be consoled, as to console;*
*To be understood as to understand;*
*To be loved as to love.*
*For it is in giving that we receive;*
*It is in pardoning that we are pardoned;*
*And it is in dying to ourselves that we are born*
*to eternal life.*

*Amen.*

# Teen Angel

"I'm closing the phone banks early," Mr. Spector announced. "Consider it a Christmas bonus."

Angie looked at her watch: four o'clock and already dark—or nearly so. This day couldn't end soon enough. The company might call it their "Customer Service Department," but to Angie it was the "Complaint Department." All day long, she listened to complaints from people who were displeased with the products they had ordered or upset because the order hadn't arrived yet. "It's Christmas, for heaven's sake," one woman yelled. "How can we even have Christmas without the set of—and clearly she was reading from the catalog—'electronic around-the-neck wine glass holders with sparkling lights in Christmas colors' that I ordered four weeks ago? They were to be the *pièce de résistance* of our holiday gathering."

Angie checked the order status, offered the company's regrets, but reminded the woman that she had actually placed the order only four days ago, with no guarantee of arrival by Christmas.

"You're clearly mistaken," the woman said and hung up. Angie moved on to the next complaint.

An hour might not be much of a bonus, but Angie wasn't about to turn it down. She left before the phone could ring again.

It wasn't as if she had to hurry home. Danny was working the late shift on Christmas Eve, Christmas Day, New Year's Eve, and New Year's Day. "Every holiday?" Angie asked.

"Most of them, but only for a year or two. The new guys always get holidays." He gave her a squeeze. "We can't leave the city unprotected."

It was only one of the problems she faced as a cop's wife. They'd been married for only a few months, and this was their first Christmas as a married couple. Angie planned to make a special breakfast on Christmas Day before Danny went to bed. Then he'd go back to work Christmas night. It wasn't the Christmas she had imagined, but Danny loved his job, and Angie loved Danny.

Angie took the long way home along Fourth Street and past St. Vincent's. Music from the church's pipe organ cascaded out of the sanctuary. Light made the stained-glass windows glow. The first Christmas Eve service had begun. I'm too late, Angie decided, but she lingered outside for a minute or two imagining the scene inside. Maybe I'll return for the eight o'clock, she thought, or the eleven. Maybe.

She didn't zip past. She stopped long enough to admire the statues that lined the walkway to the church's big wooden doors. Usually crowds made that impossible. This special exhibit had attracted people from all over the city, especially during the business day. The local news had featured the story of a wealthy donor who had given the church six angels molded in white resin. The church agreed to allow the city's best-known artists to decorate them. "The Painted Angels," they were called. Six of the Painted Angels stood along the church's front walk. Angie studied first one and then another. There was a ruby-red angel, a blue angel, a child angel, a rainbow angel, an angel holding a cat and a dog, and a granny angel.

A seventh angel stood slightly apart from the rest. It was not as magnificent as the others. A simple sign below it read: *This angel was created by the St. Vincent Youth Fellowship.*

It was a teen angel.

Angie studied it. The teen angel looked almost real. She wore jeans and a sweatshirt. She carried a backpack. The kids had painted dangly earrings on her and added a small butterfly tattoo. There was even a cell phone sticking out of the angel's pocket. Teen angel looked like the kids that Angie passed on the city streets; in fact, she looked like Angie had a few years ago.

Angie looked closer. It appeared that the teen artists had not quite finished painting the cell phone. Where there should have been a cell number, there was only white space. Angie glanced around. She was alone, totally alone. She rummaged around in her purse and pulled out a marker. She carefully wrote her own cell number in the space. "There," she said, and stuffing the marker back in her purse, she headed home.

Later, Angie wondered what had made her do it. She wasn't the kind of person who wrote in library books or sprayed graffiti on city walls. Some odd compulsion had come over her. She'd done it without even thinking.

Angie changed out of her work clothes and made a grilled cheese sandwich. The phone rang around six o'clock. Angie smiled. It had to be Danny. She grabbed it and practically yelled into the phone, "Danny!"

No one spoke.

"Danny?" Angie asked.

"Yes. Did you know I'd call?"

Surprise left Angie speechless. It wasn't her Danny on the phone. It was just a kid. Wrong number.

But before she could tell him that, he said, "I saw you outside the church. Dad let me use his phone, but he said I shouldn't expect an answer. 'It's just a statue,' he said. But I said, 'No, that's a real number on that phone, and I think it's a message from God—or maybe even Mom'—so he let me call. And I was right, wasn't I? I called and you answered."

"Right," Angie said. She had no idea what to do next. She didn't want to disappoint the kid, but she didn't want to mislead him either.

During that brief pause, the boy said, "I wanted to ask about my mom."

"Your mom?"

"Carla Bekker. Gran said that I shouldn't worry, that she was in a good place—that in heaven love abounds—but even so, I can't help wondering how she is doing."

"Your mom?" Angie repeated.

"Yah. She died last summer, so Gran came to live with us, but I miss Mom. I really do."

"Right," Angie said. "I'm sure you do. But your mom wouldn't want you to worry. You know that, don't you?" It was something her grandmother had told her years ago when grandpa died. "Worry won't bring her back."

"You're right. Mom said I should help Dad and Gran and Elsa (she's my sister) and that I shouldn't feel bad about being happy."

"Sounds like good advice to me," Angie said.

"Is she doing okay?" asked Danny, hopefully.

"Sure," Angie said—because what else could she say? "But you should do what she said. You know? Help your family and be happy. I mean, it's Christmas. We should all be happy."

"Thanks," the boy said. "I gotta go. Boy, is Dad gonna be surprised."

No more surprised than me, Angie thought, as soon as the boy broke the connection. . .

And then the phone rang again.

"Hello?" The voice was tentative. A woman, Angie thought, about my age, maybe younger.

"Hi."

"Angel?"

"Angie."

"Oh."

"Can I help you?" The words were out of her mouth before Angie even realized it. They were the exact words she used at Customer Service.

"Maybe. I don't know whether to forgive Alex or not. He says he's sorry. He says it will never happen again."

"Do you believe him?" Angie asked.

"I don't think so. He's made promises before."

Angie sighed. She probably should ask for details, but she didn't really want to know more. If there was one thing she had learned in Customer Service, it was to listen. Two things actually: to listen and to wait. She waited.

"I don't think he can stop. Not even if he wants to."

Angie waited.

The girl spoke again. "You're right. I can't forgive him. Not this time. I know what the Bible says, that we should forgive our enemies and turn the other cheek, but that hasn't worked. Not with Alex."

"Do you have someplace to go?" Angie asked.

"My parents'. They don't even know where I am, but I know they want me to come home."

"Then go to them," Angie said. "Now. Before you change your mind."

"But it's Christmas. I can't go without a gift."

"Just go," Angie said, more certain than ever that this was the right answer. "You'll be the gift. Do you have a way to get there?"

"Yes. If I leave now, I'll be there by morning." Then the caller was quiet, but she hadn't hung up.

"Thank you, Angel," she whispered and then disconnected.

Angie collapsed onto the sofa. She prayed. She prayed for the boy, Danny, and for the girl, whoever she might be. And she prayed that if the phone rang again, she'd know what to say.

But it didn't ring, and when Angie looked at the clock, she realized that if she didn't hurry, she wouldn't make the eight o'clock church service. She was far too exhausted to stay up for the eleven o'clock service.

It was raining by the time Angie left. She joined the crowd at the church's entrance. She rushed past the angels lining the walk. . .until she came to the last one, the teen angel.

Teen Angel was smiling. Had she been smiling before? The little angel still wore earrings, sported a tattoo, and clutched the cell phone, but the space where Angie had written her number was blank, just as it had been before. Angie's number had vanished, washed away in the rain. She felt a strange mixture of relief and regret as she entered the sanctuary and bowed her head in prayer.

The service was uplifting. Many in the crowd wore red, silver, or green—Christmas colors. Children squirmed and parents shushed them. Angie joined in singing the familiar carols, especially one. It's been her favorite ever since.

> *Hark the herald angels sing*
> *"Glory to the newborn King!*
> *Peace on earth and mercy mild*
> *God and sinners reconciled."*

# Praying for Holly

I t was a balmy Saturday afternoon in early December when the Randalls went to get their Christmas tree from the Boy Scouts' lot beside Knox Presbyterian Church.

"It's a family tradition," Dad said. Will, his sister Lily, Mom, and Dad piled into the car.

The lot was crowded, but that didn't stop Dad from inspecting a dozen or more trees. He kicked the base of each trunk, and either nodded or frowned, which reminded Will of Dad kicking tires before he bought the new car.

Mom checked the needles. She brushed her hand back and forth, back and forth, to see if any needles dropped off. "You know what all those needles do to my vacuum," she said.

Lily named each tree: "It looks like a Chloe," she would say thoughtfully, or "Definitely a Fluffy." (Will had no idea how a tree could look like "a Chloe," and there was certainly nothing fluffy about a spruce tree, but that was Lily's contribution.)

"Am I the only sane person in this family?" Will asked. "They all look good to me."

Eventually, they agreed on a tree. When Dad dragged it into the living room, Will noticed a small piece of plastic wrapped around one of the branches about halfway up, deep in the tree where the branch met the trunk. At first he didn't think much about it, but when his father went to get tools to fix the tree stand, Will reached in and yanked the thing off the branch. He pulled hard, and the rubber band, which had been holding the plastic to the trunk, snapped. Will fell backward onto the couch, a sandwich bag in his hand. He stared at it. There was something inside.

Will gently pulled out a piece of paper and unfolded it. The letters, written in pencil, were smudged. Will read the message: *My name is Holly Praska. I am 10 years old. I live with my mother in Chelm, Wisconsin. We cut Christmas trees for extra money. I hope you like this one. I think it's pretty. Please pray for us. —Holly*

Will reread the message. Twice.

A girl named Holly had cut down his tree. She was ten, just like him. He'd never thought much about where the trees had been before the Boy Scouts got them. Now he knew: His tree came from Wisconsin. And a girl named Holly had gone into the forest to cut it down.

He studied the tree. It was taller than he was, and he was tall for ten.

Holly must be strong and smart. Will didn't know how to cut down a tree. He didn't even know if tree cutters used saws or axes. Maybe they used lasers. It was all a mystery.

Then Will considered the rest of the message: *please pray for us.*

That confused him even more. Why did Holly need prayers? Maybe she was in trouble. Maybe she was sick, or her mom was. She didn't mention her dad. Did he cut trees too? Was he there in Wisconsin with Holly and her mom? Or were they all alone?

Will had never known a kid his age who asked for prayers. He'd certain never done it.

"Prayer makes a difference," Grandpa always said at the end of a visit, "so keep praying for me." That made sense. Grandpa was as old as the dinosaurs, so he needed prayers to survive.

Will figured that Mom and Dad would do whatever praying Grandpa needed, and it was probably a lot.

Will shoved the note into his pocket. For some reason he couldn't explain, he wanted to keep the note secret. It was as if Holly had reached out to him, to another kid her own age, and he didn't feel like telling anyone about it.

Thoughts of Holly stayed in Will's mind that day, the next day, and all during the weeks leading up to Christmas. He thought of her when he was in church on Sundays, and he tried to pray for her like she asked, but since he didn't know what exactly Holly needed, his thoughts wandered. He imagined what Holly looked like—dark hair, maybe, in pigtails, wearing a heavy coat and boots and swinging an ax at a tree. It seemed unlikely she would own a laser. "Dear God, keep Holly safe," he prayed. "Axes are dangerous."

But he wasn't sure that was the right prayer.

The next Sunday he tried again. Pastor Fernsby prayed out loud for the victims of an earthquake. Apparently, praying for something specific was the way to go, but what did Holly need?

"Dear God, help Holly survive the earthquake," he prayed. Luckily he prayed silently because he realized too late that the earthquake had been in India, not in Wisconsin. "Dear God, not the earthquake. . .it's something else. I don't know what."

But what good is a prayer if it isn't specific? Will wondered how God would know what Holly and her mother really needed if he didn't supply enough details.

Holly began haunting his thoughts, day and night. There must be something more he could do for her than just pray, something more practical.

He wished he could write or call or send her an email, but he didn't even know her address.

Holly was on Will's mind that Christmas Eve when he slid into a pew at Knox Presbyterian with his family. But he almost forgot her in all the hubbub of the family candlelight service. Pastor Fernsby read the nativity story from the Bible, and between each passage the congregation sang familiar Christmas carols. "It Came Upon a Midnight Clear" was one of Will's favorites. He imagined Holly and her mom standing on a hillside beneath a starry sky, surrounded by the stumps of what were now Christmas trees.

When the organist began to play another hymn, "While Shepherds Watched their Flocks by Night," Will stopped thinking about Holly. Instead, he thought about those shepherds. The angels said, "Do not be afraid," so the shepherds must have been scared at first, really scared. But after the angels told them about the baby, the shepherds did exactly what they were supposed to do. Even so, they must have been confused. They didn't really know why God wanted them to visit the baby lying in a manger. "Maybe they were as confused by God's request as I am about Holly's," Will thought.

And the wise men? Had they been confused too? They followed a star believing that's what God wanted them to do. They didn't seem confused. They just obeyed. None of the Bible people knew the details, and they sure didn't know how the story would end. They just did their best to follow God's commands.

"Maybe God expects me to just pray and trust that he knows what Holly needs." Will felt a great peace settle upon him. "Yes," he realized. "God already knows. He doesn't need me to provide details."

The next day, when the family paused for grace before Christmas dinner, Will asked, "Can we pray for a friend of mine?"

"What friend is that?" Mom asked.

"A girl named Holly. And her mother. Both of them."

"Is that someone from school? I've never heard that name before. Who is she?"

"Just someone. I don't know much about her, only that she needs prayer. Let's just do it."

"Of course," Dad said. "Go ahead."

Will bowed his head and prayed: "Dear God, bless our family and friends, we pray, and bless all those we know really well, and while you're at it, please bless those we've never even met, like Holly and her mother, because you know them even if we don't. In the name of Jesus, Amen."

# The Holiday Bus

Nora shifted into low gear as the yellow school bus began the climb up Turtle Hill Road. The twenty-eight kids already on the bus were quiet—dreaming, perhaps, of holiday parties. Nora noticed the Christmas red of hair ribbons, socks, and shirt collars poking out from under winter jackets. Lisa Bowman cradled a box of red frosted cupcakes in her lap. Several kids were hauling bags of potato chips or cans of red juice.

Nora appreciated the moment's silence. Once the Ludlows clambered aboard, the bus would become a zoo. "Strength, Lord, and patience," she prayed, "and courage for dealing with the Ludlows." Jesus taught his followers to love the little children, and that included the Ludlows.

As the school year progressed, Nora found it increasingly difficult to love the Ludlows. Nora vowed not to lose the battle, not today, the day before Christmas break. God knew she tried. Nora treated the Ludlows like the others—a smile when they boarded, a friendly word as they unloaded, candy once in a while, and a hug on birthdays. Nora loved kids—at least normal ones. Why else would she drive school bus? Not the salary. Not the hours. Not the working conditions! Nora looked at the small magnet she'd stuck on the dashboard: "If God gives you lemons, make lemonade." God gave Ludlows to Nora. What could she make of them?

There was Derek, Dudley, Darla, and Daisy. Two boys, two girls, and she understood that there were four more *D* babies at home. Derek, Dudley, Darla, and Daisy got on the bus with hair uncombed, and Nora concluded that washcloths and soap were as lacking as combs and brushes. All four wore clothes that didn't fit well. Common sense told Nora that Derek's "too small" could have been Dudley's "just right," but the Ludlows seemed unaware of that possibility.

In September, when Daisy had a bad case of school phobia, Nora gave her a small package—hair ribbons, something Daisy could show off proudly to classmates. Daisy had taken the package eagerly, but Nora never saw her wear the ribbons in her unruly hair. The week before Halloween, Nora had handed Derek a bag of apples. He snatched it and quickly ran into the house. Nora kept track of the birthdays of each child who rode her bus, and when Darla celebrated her eighth in early November, Nora had given her a new eight-pack of Crayolas and a drawing pad. Darla smiled shyly but never said a word.

Nora was particularly fond of Thanksgiving. She loved the smells of autumn and the chill in the air that made coming indoors so comforting. It was more than that, though. She loved the very idea of thankfulness. She sang "Come, Ye Thankful People, Come" so often that all the children on the bus, even the very little ones, could sing along. Gazing at her passengers in the rear-view window, Nora thought she saw Darla singing, but she couldn't be sure. Perhaps it was simply wishful thinking.

The last day before the Thanksgiving holiday, Nora presented each child with a treat: a maple sugar Pilgrim wrapped in orange tissue paper. "Oh," said the children, delighted because most of them had never tasted maple sugar candy before. Nora had purchased the treats on a summer vacation because they reminded her of her own New England childhood. Every single child said "thank you," except the Ludlows. They just took.

Still Nora tried. She "oohed and aahed" over Derek's and Dudley's show-and-tells. To date: one snake, two frogs, a supposedly uninhabited hornets' nest, and a knife, which they claimed they had "got off a dead man." Nora had admired all from a safe distance and confiscated the knife.

The bus pulled to a stop in front of the Ludlow house. Nora beeped the horn.

Derek stuck his head out the Ludlows' door. "Hold your horses! We're just finishing somethin'."

A minute or two later all four Ludlows tumbled from the house and ran toward the bus.

"Good morning," Nora said in her friendliest voice. As usual, there was no reply.

Nora closed the door, checked to see that the children were seated, and shifted the bus into drive. The bus got noisier, and Nora heard a shrill cry.

"Daisy's bleeding," Dudley yelled. "You better do somethin'."

"She'll be fine," Nora said. "We're almost to school."

"Lots of blood back here," Derek called. "How much blood does a person got?"

Nora pulled the bus to a stop because, with the Ludlows, she was never certain. She grabbed her first aid kit and hustled to the back of the bus.

There was a tiny trickle of blood on Daisy's finger where a scab had been pried loose. Nora applied a Snoopy bandaid to the grimy pinky. "You'll be fine," she said before returning to the driver's seat. She put the bus into gear and pulled back onto the highway.

When they arrived at school, Nora parked the bus, and the kids piled off.

The Ludlows were last. Derek, Darla, and Daisy walked past Nora without a word. Dudley stopped and said, "There's somethin' on that seat in the back."

"Thanks for telling me," Nora said. Whatever it was probably smelled bad.

"Wacha gonna do about it?" Dudley asked.

"I'll check it."

Dudley seemed satisfied. He jumped to the ground.

Nora walked down the aisle. On the seat was a package wrapped in newspaper and tied together with bailing twine. Nora lifted it gingerly. It looked almost like a gift.

Every time she received a gift, she tried to guess what was inside, but this time she simply shook her head. She wasn't sure it *was* a gift. With the Ludlows, anything was possible.

She carried the crude package to the front of the bus and used the small scissors in the first aid kit to cut the string. The paper fell open to reveal four pine cones tied together with striped hair ribbons, the very ones she had given Daisy in September. A piece of paper from Darla's drawing pad bore a crayoned greeting: *We made this pine cone thing for your tree. Thank you for being our friend.*

Below the message, all four children had signed their names—four illegible *D* names. Nora draped the pine cone decoration on the rearview mirror so that the children would notice it when she picked them up after school.

As she pulled the bus out of the schoolyard, she glanced in the rearview mirror. Between the dangling pine cones she spotted the Ludlow children trudging up the big stone steps into the school. "Thank you, God, for giving me Ludlows," Nora prayed, and she meant it.

# The Manchesters' Christmas Photo

R oger Anderson gently tugged at the bundle of Christmas cards clogging his mail slot. As always, Christmas Eve was the biggest mail day of the year at the Andersons' Arizona apartment. Roger missed the white Christmases of North Dakota, but after he had retired, Nan insisted they spend winters in a warm place. "After all," she had said, "there are so many North Dakotans in Arizona that we'll feel right at home." So each year from then on, right after Halloween, they relocated near friends in Mesa. In their hearts, though, they missed family and friends left behind, and eagerly anticipated notes and pictures that came with Christmas cards.

"Thank God some people still send cards," Roger said.

"The old ways are still the best," Nan said gratefully each time a card arrived.

Roger handed the mail to Nan, who quickly separated the cards and letters from the bills and

junk mail. While Roger poured them both steam-
ing cups of coffee, Nan settled into the rocker
with the cards.

"Oh, look," she said, handing one of the photo
cards to Roger. "It's from the Manchesters!"

Roger looked over Nan's shoulder. For years he
and Nan had driven over to Bob and Sue Manchesters' farm every Thanksgiving evening, for pie
and for Roger to take a photo for the Manchesters'
Christmas card. After Roger and Nan had moved,
someone else took over snapping the Manchester
family photo, which made Nan happy and sad at
the same time.

In the most recent photo, the photo Roger
now held, Bob and Sue looked happier than they
had in years. The family had grown over the years
as they added spouses and grandchildren. Bob
and Sue were a bit heavier and grayer, but Nan
couldn't get over how content they all looked.

She examined the photo more closely. "Look,
Roger. In the back." She pointed to a tall man and
a smaller woman at his side. "That's Eric isn't it?"

Roger nodded. "I believe it is!"

Nan reached out and squeezed his hand, a
smile spreading across her face. How well they
remembered Eric. He'd gone to school with their
son, Tom, and the two boys had spent hours in
the garage working on one car or another. Even
then, Nan had felt a special sympathy for Eric; he

was less social and more restless than the other Manchester kids. He didn't seem to have as many friends.

Bob and Sue confided to the Andersons that their youngest son had been the most difficult of all the children. Although he was bright and clever enough, he didn't like school—he only "just got by." He didn't like sports, either. He didn't like camping and fishing or anything the rest of the family liked. Cars were his hobby. He constantly battled with his dad about staying out late and driving recklessly. Eric seldom helped around the house; Bob thought he was lazy. "There's no free lunch in this life," he told Eric, but Eric shrugged his shoulders and said nothing. He rarely spoke to his father.

"How come you'll fix everybody else's cars for nothing, but you won't take five minutes to look at my pickup?" Bob would ask.

Eric said, "I've got more important stuff to do," and then he'd leave, letting the screen door slam shut behind him.

Eric went to trade school to study auto mechanics. As it turned out, he already knew everything they tried to teach him, so he dropped out before the winter term began.

He drifted for a few months, and then he joined the Army. Bob and Sue were pleased. They hoped the Army would teach him initiative and discipline.

After basic training in New Jersey, Eric was stationed in Korea. Korea seemed so far-off and mysterious that the assignment had troubled Bob and Sue. But they decided that if Eric could find some purpose for his life while in Korea, it would be the answer to their prayers.

The Army recognized Eric's mechanical skills and put him to work repairing helicopters. He wrote home from time to time. The letters were brief and friendly; he told them that he was using his free time to travel around the countryside. He said he was learning Korean.

Bob had told Roger that it seemed strange that Eric was learning Korean, such a difficult language. There certainly wasn't any evidence from his teenage years that Eric could even speak English properly, no less possess the ability to learn Korean. Even so, Bob was pleased that Eric was taking advantage of his time overseas to try new and different things.

After two years in Korea, Eric returned to the States to spend Thanksgiving weekend with the family. Everyone thought he'd be there for the Christmas photo.

The weekend had gone well. Everyone was glad to see Eric. Later, Sue told Nan that Eric had matured. He'd been polite and more serious about life. He pitched in to help and spoke pleasantly about his travels. He showed interest in the lives of his brothers and sisters, and enjoyed playing with the nieces and nephews. "Bob and I were so relieved," she said. They felt, Sue admitted, like so many parents who have patiently endured a child's teenage years and realize for the first time that it has been worth all the heartache and worry. Everything was going to be all right.

"But we rejoiced too soon," she admitted to Nan later as she told what happened next. After dinner Eric took his parents aside and said, "Mom, Dad, I've got something important to tell you. I've fallen in love with a Korean girl, and we're going to be married."

"I didn't say anything," Sue admitted, "at least not at first."

Bob said he hoped that Eric would think carefully before he did something foolish. "Love can blind a person to what's sensible. It'll be hard for a Korean girl to feel at home so far from her own family and culture."

"We're not going to stay here," Eric said. "I can live better as a mechanic in Korea than I can here. We'll be living in Korea."

"I tried desperately not to cry," Sue admitted. "Bob told him, 'You can't just throw your life away like that.'"

"I'm not throwing my life away. I've never been happier. My life is in Korea now. I'm respected there, and there's nothing for me here. Never was."

"What do you mean by that remark?" Bob shouted. "Your mother and I have given you a good home and a Christian upbringing."

"There are Christians in Korea," Eric countered.

"They're not family. I will not let you do this."

Eric turned away. "I'm sorry you feel that way, but I'm leaving."

"Please stay," Sue pleaded as Eric hurried to his car.

Bob stood at the door and yelled at him. The words were mean and hurtful, although later Bob could not recall exactly what he had said. Perhaps he forgot because he was embarrassed by his harsh words. After all, Bob was a good and kind man. But even the best people can have vicious reactions when the wrong buttons are pushed; touch those buttons and ugly things come out.

There was no Manchester family Christmas photo that year. When Roger and Nan arrived with their camera, Sue said she didn't have the heart for a photograph, and Bob was too angry to talk. It wasn't until weeks later that Sue revealed to Nan the details of Eric's departure.

Later, when Bob finally told Roger all that had transpired on that fateful Thanksgiving, Bob shook his head and said, "I don't know how I let it get so out of control. I'll always regret that terrible day." He confided to Roger that there were times, especially in the early morning, when he was alone in the barn that he could almost hear the shouts of a much younger Eric running from the house. Sometimes in church he'd confess to God the thoughtlessness of the words he'd spoken. The pain was almost too much to bear. Sometimes he'd look up at the stars in the sky and wonder if Eric, looking skyward in Korea, might at that moment be looking at the same ones.

Roger tried to console his friend Bob, but words failed. "Nan and I are praying for Eric," he'd say, but he wasn't sure that prayers could mend this rift. Bob could not relive that fateful Thanksgiving night nor take back those terrible words. But life goes on.

The next year Roger took a photo, a rather good one, he felt, but, of course, Eric was no longer in the picture – literally or figuratively. Roger took seven more Manchester Christmas photos in the years before he and Nan moved to Arizona. By then, no one mentioned Eric's absence, but Roger and Nan often thought about him and prayed for the family's reconciliation.

Nan had tears in her eyes as she looked at the latest Manchester Christmas photo. "You read it," she said to Roger. "I'm not seeing clearly."

"We're seeing an answer to prayer," Roger said as he studied the photo. He noticed that Eric's left hand rested gently on the shoulder of the petite woman standing beside him. Above her picture, Sue had written *Choi, Eric's wife.* A boy, who looked to be about six-years-old, sat on the ground a row or two in front of Eric and Choi. Beneath his picture, Sue had written *Kyu-Hyung, our grandson.* Roger turned the picture over. On the back Sue had written in her neat hand: *The Lord gives strength to his people; the Lord blesses his people with peace. —Psalm 29:11.*

Roger put the card down on the table beside Nan's rocker. She saw that he also had tears in his eyes. "Merry Christmas," he said. "And God bless."

# Hanima's Hands

The fifth-grade Sunday school class was a good bunch of kids. Most of them had been together since kindergarten. The only newcomer was Hanima, who came for the first time that fall.

Hanima was quiet and seemed nervous on that first day. She sat by herself. Mrs. Preston, the teacher, tried to include her. She asked how long Hanima had been in town.

"Since summer," the girl answered.

"Where did you use to live?"

"Far away," she said, her eyes downward.

"And what's your name?"

"Hanima."

"Hanima. That's a beautiful name," Mrs. Preston said. "What does it mean?"

"I don't know," the girl said. "It's just a name."

"Well, it's a very pretty name. And please feel free to take your lovely gloves off and stay."

But Hanima didn't take her gloves off that first day, or any day. Hanima always wore gloves. Usually they were white or black, sometimes blue or light green. They were thin gloves that didn't stop her from writing, doing craft projects, or turning the pages of the Bible. She knew the Bible very well, far better than most of the kids in the class. But she never removed her gloves.

From time to time kids would ask why she wore them. Most of the time she'd shrug and say nothing at all. Sometimes, she'd simply say, "I just want to." And because she spoke with quiet firmness, after a while the kids stopped asking. But they never stopped wondering: what's the deal with Hanima's hands?

Now, to appreciate fully what happened in church that Christmas Eve, you need to know what the kids in Mrs. Preston's class didn't know about Hanima's hands. In her old country Hanima worked with her mother at home to support the family, as many of the village children did. They worked with carpets. After school Hanima would hurry home and go to work. And every day Hanima's fingers dealt with poisonous dyes and sharp knives. The dye turned her hands an ugly purplish color. The knives left scars. She was not ashamed of having helped her family, but she was ashamed of her hands. Hanima wore gloves to hide the marks.

Teachers at school understood. The Sunday school kids might have understood, too, if someone had told them. They certainly would have stopped giving her curious stares, but no one thought to explain.

On the first Sunday in December Mrs. Preston announced to the class that they'd be staging the nativity pageant as part of the Christmas Eve service. Hanima would play the role of Mary. The other kids saw at once what Mrs. Preston was doing. She was trying to draw Hanima out of her shyness, to get her involved, help her feel accepted, and it seemed to work. Hanima smiled, a big natural smile, unlike anything they'd seen from her.

But you could have heard a candle drip when Mrs. Preston said, "Now, Hanima, you can't do this with gloves on. We try to be as authentic as possible, and the Virgin Mary wouldn't have worn gloves, that's for sure."

"I can't do it, then. I am sorry. Thank you very much, but I prefer not to do it." Hanima looked down.

So Mrs. Preston gave the role of Mary to Anna. Hanima became the innkeeper's wife, in the same sort of simple dress Mary wore. Hanima held a dish towel to hide her hands. It was as though she'd been working in the kitchen, which pleased Hanima.

The other students were assigned their parts. A boy, who happened to be named Joseph, although everyone called him Joey, took the role of Joseph. Mrs. Preston was satisfied with the rehearsals.

But on Christmas Eve, as the children were lining up at the back of the church to begin the pageant, Anna's face turned white.

"I feel nauseous." She dashed toward the bathroom.

Mrs. Preston slumped forward. What to do? The organist had already begun playing "O Little Town of Bethlehem." This was the moment when Mary and Joseph were supposed to walk down the aisle to the manger at the front of the sanctuary.

Mrs. Preston looked at the remaining children, who were dressed as shepherds, angels, and wise men. Only Hanima was wearing a simple dress like Mary would have worn. "Quick, Hanima, you'll have to be Mary," Mrs. Preston said. "Take off your gloves and get going."

Mrs. Preston's request was so urgent that Hanima yanked off the gloves, first one, then the other, and tossed them on a nearby table without a second thought.

The children milling around saw her hands for the first time. They couldn't hide their shock. "What happened?" one of them asked.

"Gross," said another, and she felt bad the moment she said it.

Hanima looked as if she was about to cry. She hid her hands behind her back, but it was too late to pretend her hands were perfect: the gloves were off. Mrs. Preston grabbed Hanima's hand, placed it on Joey's arm, and pushed the two of them down the aisle.

"Go, go, go, go, go."

And they did. Hanima walked down the aisle, one hand shakily resting on Joey's arm, the other hidden in the folds of her dress. When they got to the manger, they sat down on the bale of hay that Mrs. Preston had placed there. Hanima hid her hands in her lap.

Three-month-old Olivia Townshend had been chosen to play baby Jesus. Olivia's mother expected Anna to be waiting to take Olivia and was surprised to find Hanima instead. Mrs. Townshend never met Hanima, but she trusted Mrs. Preston so she bent down to place the baby in Hanima's hands.

Hanima smiled, brought her hands forward, and opened them wide. Mrs. Townshend gently placed her beautiful, precious baby into Hanima's waiting hands. The baby looked up and smiled at Hanima, and Hanima grinned back.

I won't say everything was perfect for Hanima from that moment on. It's tough, being the new kid. And when you're from another country and speak in a foreign accent, it's even harder. However, something wonderful happened that Christmas Eve, something Hanima could never explain.

She came to the manger scared and went away brave. She came feeling alone in the world and went away with friends. She came embarrassed about who she was and left knowing that no matter what she looks like, no matter what others may think, she will always be a beloved child of God.

# The Holy Night

**Based on a classic story by Selma Lagerlöf**

Once upon a time a man went out in the dark and cold to borrow some live coals to kindle a fire. He went from one little hut to another. He planned to say, "Kind friends, help me! My wife has just given birth, and I want to build a fire to warm her and our new child."

But it was late in the night, and everyone was sleeping. No one answered his knock.

The man walked on in the darkness. After a while he saw a glimmer of firelight in the distance. He walked toward it. As he got closer, he saw that the fire was burning in an open meadow. A great many sheep were lying around it, sleeping. An old shepherd sat by the fire watching them.

When the man came close to the sheep, several fierce dogs sprang up. They opened their great jaws widely as if to bark, but no sound came forth. Their sharp white teeth glistened in the firelight, and the hair along their backs bristled as they prepared to attack. They leaped on him. One bit his foot. One sunk his teeth into the man's hand, and the other clung to his throat. The man shook with fear until he realized that the dogs' ferocious jaws and teeth did not break his skin. He remained unscathed. The dogs slinked away.

The man intended to approach the fire, but the sheep were huddled so closely together that they formed a barrier between him and it. The only way to get there was to walk right over the sheep. The man began stepping on the backs of one sheep after another. The sheep never woke. They never even shifted in their sleep.

When the man reached the fire, the shepherd picked up his sharp spiked staff. He used it to tend the sheep, but this time he aimed it directly at the stranger's head. The staff soared toward the man. He did not have time to duck, but he didn't need to. Just before it reached its target, the staff turned away of its own accord and sailed harmlessly into the meadow.

The man approached the shepherd and said, "My friend, won't you help me and give me some of your fire? My wife has just given birth, and I want to build a fire to warm her and our new child."

The shepherd would normally have refused, but he remembered that the dogs could not bite the man, the sheep had not awakened, and the staff had veered away from the man's head. Gruffly, he said, "Take as much as you wish."

The fire had nearly burned out. There were no logs left, only a heap of glowing coals. The man had no shovel or pail in which to carry coals. So, he picked them up with his fingers. He laid them in the folds of his cloak. They neither burned his fingers nor scorched his cloak. He carried them as easily as if they had been nuts or apples.

The shepherd, amazed, asked, "Will you tell me what kind of night this is when dogs cannot bite, sheep do not wake, a staff won't kill, and fire does not scorch?"

The man answered, "That I cannot tell you if you do not see with your own eyes." He turned away, for he wished to return to his wife and child as quickly as possible to give them warmth and light.

The shepherd had never encountered such strange events. It was perplexing. It was troubling. He followed the man, hoping to learn what these strange signs might mean.

At last they came to the place where the man lived. It was a poor, lowly abode—a bare cave in the side of the mountain with a dirt floor and rock walls.

Even though the shepherd was by nature a cruel and unkind man, he felt pity for the young couple. He removed the knapsack from his shoulders and took out a wooly white lambskin. "Here," he said as he handed it to the stranger. "Let the little child sleep on this."

When the shepherd completed this one act of kindness, his eyes were opened, and he was amazed. The cave no longer appeared bare and empty. A ring of silver-winged angels formed a ring around the baby, and each was playing an instrument and singing a joyful song about a baby born this very night:

> *Joy to the world! The Lord is come;*
> *Let earth receive her King;*
> *Let every heart prepare him room,*
> *And heaven and nature sing,*
> *And heaven and nature sing,*
> *And heaven, and heaven, and nature sing.*

From that moment on, the shepherd became a different man—a kinder, gentler man. He sought ways to help others even before they asked for help because living in God's light enabled him to hear heaven and nature sing.

Angels came to earth on the first Christmas Eve. And they come every Christmas Eve, if we know how to find them. We don't need the light of lamps or candles or moon or stars. We simply need to have the right kind of eyes, eyes wide open to the world around us, and hearts willing to help others.

# Day Care Christmas Eve

Snow began to fall at nine o'clock in the morning on Christmas Eve day. The children at Good Shepherd Day Care, busy making Christmas cookies, didn't notice it until Nick, licking frosting off his fingers, looked out the window and yelled, "Snow!"

Everyone ran to the windows. Snow covered the playground, the parking lot, and the plastic poinsettias on the church lawn.

"Can we build snow people?" a child asked.

"Can we go sledding?" asked another as they stumbled into their snowsuits, snow boots, and mittens.

They played in the snow until they were shivery cold.

When they came inside, Mrs. Helper, their teacher, turned on the weather report, while Mrs. Angel, the assistant teacher, helped the children hang up their wet clothes.

They all stopped to listen as the radio announcer said, "A surprise snowstorm hit the metro area this morning, and snow is still falling. Expect delays going home."

"Will we be delayed going home?" Hannah asked.

Mrs. Helper's mouth smiled, but her eyes looked worried. "We may," she said. "Let's wait and see."

By noon moms, dads, grandmas, grandpas, and big brothers and sisters began to arrive at Good Shepherd Day Care Center.

"Work let out early," they said. "We tried to beat the storm."

One by one the children went home. Every time a child left, the waiting got harder for those who remained. "I'm tired of waiting," Ella said, and Amelia, her twin sister, added, "Me, too."

"We're all tired of waiting," Logan said, and the day care children nodded in agreement.

It seemed as if they had been waiting for one thing or another all year long. In September, Mrs. Angel announced that she was going to have a baby in December. The children waited and waited, and there was still no Angel baby. "Soon," Mrs. Angel said.

At the beginning of December, they began waiting for Christmas. Mrs. Helper called the Christmas waiting *Advent*. "Waiting is an important part of Christmas," she said. "We use this time to get ready."

"But *we're* already ready," the children said.

Mrs. Helper just smiled.

By two o'clock on Christmas Eve only seven children were left at Good Shepherd Day Care.

"When can *we* go home?" the twins, Ella and Amelia, asked at the same exact time.

Little Jake began to cry. He clutched his special blanket to his chest and sucked on the worn blue blanket fuzz. Hannah, his big sister, told him not to worry. "Mommy will come," she said, and she hoped it was true. Waiting was very hard even for the bigger boys and girls.

Mrs. Angel set up the easels for painting. As the children put on their paint smocks, the phone began to ring.

First to call was Hannah and Jake's mom. "I'm stuck in traffic," she said.

Then Logan's dad called. "I can't get through the storm," he said. "I've never seen it so bad. The police have closed many of the highways, and they are warning everyone to stay off the roads. They've stopped plowing. Even the emergency vehicles can't get through."

Mrs. Helper assured him that the children would be fine. "We'll take good care of them. Please don't worry." Clearly, the *day care* was going to be *night care* thanks to the storm.

"I can't get out until the snowplow comes by," the twins' grandmother said when she called, and

Kyle's mom and Jenna's dad both called to say they would be late too. "Snow," one said. "The traffic is not moving," said the other.

Mrs. Helper told them not to worry. "We're snug and cozy at day care."

Around three o'clock the minister of Good Shepherd Church, Pastor Jenkins, stopped by to check on the day care children. "The church is toasty warm," he told them. "Come on up if you get chilly in the day care rooms. No Christmas Eve this year."

"No Christmas Eve?" Logan exclaimed, "You can't cancel Christmas Eve!"

Pastor Jenkins smiled and put a kindly arm around Logan's shoulder. "You're absolutely right, young man. Christmas comes every year no matter what the weather. What I canceled was the Christmas Eve *church service*. It's too stormy for people to come out on a night like tonight."

At four o'clock Mrs. Angel's husband came in the door looking like a snowman. He shook fluffy flakes all over the floor. "Yo, ho, ho," he called. "Merry Christmas!"

The children ran over and hugged his knees. "It's a good thing you have a big truck," Logan said.

Mr. Angel agreed. "Even my big truck had trouble getting through this storm. I think we're stranded here for the night."

Mrs. Angel looked worried. "Oh, Joe," she said to her husband, "I just felt a twinge. I think the baby's going to be born tonight. Can we make it to the hospital?"

"Even the ambulance won't get through in this storm," Mr. Angel said. "The main roads are closed."

"Oh, my stars!" Mrs. Helper exclaimed. "The baby? Now?"

The children cheered. "The baby's coming! The baby's coming!"

"I'm glad someone's pleased," Mrs. Helper said. "Logan, go find Pastor Jenkins."

Logan ran to the church office.

Mrs. Helper began to give orders. "Joe," she said to Mr. Angel, "you take your wife into the napping room and find her a soft place to lie down. Hannah, you'll have to keep an eye on the little ones while we grown-ups help Mrs. Angel and the baby."

Logan raced back into the main day care room with Pastor Jenkins right behind him. "I used to work on an ambulance crew," the pastor said. "Perhaps I can help with the birth. I called 911, but they don't think they can get through the storm."

All the grown-ups disappeared into the napping room.

The children stood still for a second. Everything had happened very quickly. "What shall we do?" Hannah asked.

"We can read stories," Ella suggested.

"Christmas stories," Amelia added.

They settled down in the book nook and looked at the Christmas storybooks. They showed one another their favorite pictures. It was hard to focus at first, but Hannah, Logan, and the twins acted out the stories for the smaller children, and soon they were all laughing and having fun.

After a while, though, Little Jake, Jenna, and Kyle complained they were hungry. Hannah, Logan, and the twins searched the snack cupboard and set out a supper of cheese crackers, apple juice, and the cookies they had decorated that morning, the ones that were supposed be gifts for moms and dads. They ate everything and then cleaned up the crumbs.

The day care rooms grew chilly. The heat in those rooms lowered automatically during the evening hours. Logan suggested that they go into the church. After all, Pastor Jenkins had promised that the church was toasty warm.

"We'll need a light," Ella said, and Amelia pulled out the box of Christmas candle flashlights that the children had used in their Christmas program. Hannah handed each child a battery-lit candle, and they marched single-file down the long church hall.

They marched right up to the front of the church where a manger was waiting for the baby Jesus. "This is where the big kids were going to have their pageant," Hannah explained to the little ones. "I remember it from last year. There was a Mary and Joseph, angels, shepherds, and wise men. There was even a real baby lying in the manger. He cried."

"Really?" The children approached the manger and peeked inside.

"It's empty now," Kyle said.

"No baby," Jenna said.

The children settled onto the hay that surrounded the manger. They felt very small inside the big empty church. Jenna began to cry, and everyone tried to comfort her. It was Hannah who suggested that they sing some of the Christmas carols they had learned in day care. "Singing takes away the tears," she said.

She began with "Away in a Manger." Logan joined in. So did Ella and Amelia. Soon even the little ones were singing along. They didn't know very many songs, but they sang also "Silent Night," "Jingle Bells," and "We Wish You A Merry Christmas" over and over again until they were so tired that they all fell asleep on the hay.

The children, tired as they were, slept soundly that night. If the little ones woke, a glance at their sleeping friends lulled them back to sleep quickly. They didn't stir when Mrs. Helper covered them with blankets, quilts, and comforters from the day care rooms. They didn't hear the scrape of snowplows working through the night to clear the roads and parking lots.

It was the morning sunlight streaming through the church windows that woke them. Logan sat up first, then Hannah, Ella and Amelia, Jenna, Kyle, and finally Little Jake, rubbing the sleep from his eyes. "Good morning, sleepy heads," Mrs. Helper said.

"Merry Christmas," said Pastor Jenkins.

"The baby. . .?" Hannah asked, but her question was interrupted by a tiny cry. It came from the manger.

The children rushed to peek inside. There, asleep on the hay, lay a tiny baby. "It's the Angel baby," Hannah said.

Mr. and Mrs. Angel gazed fondly at their new-born child. "We named her Mary," Mr. Angel said.

"Like Jesus's mommy," Jenna said.

"Yes, we thought it was a fine name for a Christmas baby."

The children were so busy admiring the baby that they didn't notice the commotion outside until the church doors banged open and their families poured in. Hannah and Little Jake's mom, Logan's dad, and the twins' grandparents rushed through the doors. Jenna and Kyle's mom and dad ran up the aisle to greet their children. There were hugs, kisses, and happy shouts all round until Hannah called, "Shh! The baby is sleeping."

All the moms and dads and grandparents peeked into the manger. "Lovely," they said.

"A beautiful baby."

"A gift from God."

"And on Christmas Day. . ."

"It's what Christmas is all about," Hannah said. "We waited and waited and waited, but at the end of the waiting we found the best gift of all—a baby lying in a manger. Merry Christmas. Merry Christmas to all!"

# About the Authors

Richard Raum is an ordained Presbyterian minister. He has served churches in Virginia, New York, New Jersey, Michigan, and North Dakota. Many of these stories were originally told in those churches. He is a graduate of the University of Vermont and Princeton Seminary. He taught at several colleges and also worked as a fundraiser for church-related nonprofits. He is married to Elizabeth Raum. They split their time between Fargo, North Dakota, and North Myrtle Beach, South Carolina.

Elizabeth Raum has written more than one hundred books for children, as well as a biography for adults, *Dietrich Bonhoeffer: Called by God*, published by Bloomsbury Press. Her recent books for children include the *Choose Your Journey* series of interactive Bible novels for readers ages 7-10, published by JourneyForth. To learn more, visit her Facebook page, Elizabeth Raum, Children's Author, or her website:

www.elizabethraumbooks.com.

# Additional Books
# by Elizabeth Raum

A series of Bible-based interactive novels
especially for readers ages 7-10.

# Thank you from CrossLink Publishing

**We appreciate your support of quality faith-based books. If you enjoyed this book would you consider sharing it with others?**

- Mention the book on Facebook, Twitter, Pinterest, or your blog.
- Recommend this book to your small group, book club, or work colleagues.
- Pick up a copy for someone you know who would be encouraged by this book.
- Write a review on Amazon.com, Goodreads.com or BarnesandNoble.com.
- To learn about our latest releases, check out the **Coming Soon** section of our website: CrossLinkPublishing.com

Printed in the United States
By Bookmasters